LETTERS FROM NAN

Letters from Nan

*"Call it hope or fate,
but I call it love."*

ASHLYNN JOHNSON

Ashlynn Johnson

Contents

Letters from Nan

Ashlynn Johnson fell in love with writing fiction stories that pull her readers into books filled with romance, courage, and determination. She is from Indiana where she published Love on Shore (2019) and Love is a Storm (2020).

She has a passion for helping others and using her mind to write incredible love stories that not only people can relate to, but she has encountered through personal experiences. Ashlynn graduated from the University of Southern Indiana with both a Bachelor's and Master's Degree. She contributes to many local organizations within her community and makes every effort to ensure her readers feel every emotion she puts into her writing.

Copyright © 2021

Prologue

From a very young age we are taught how to tell the difference between right and wrong. We are shown how to live and love, and when to forgive and forget.

Throughout our lives, these traits can carry us through experiences we may not understand how to navigate. Finding an anchor to help pull us back to the correct path may require a loved one showing us a new way, or providing us with enough experience to help make that choice on our own.

Fighting for what we want is always a good thing, but only if that fight does not damage those that we love in the midst of it all.

Dedication

Christmas cookie baking
Annual Mamaw Cheeseburger nights on Allen's Lane
Massive Family Easter Egg hunts
Watching Little Rascals over and over

Grandparents are very special people because they are allowed to act like kids again. They make us laugh, they show us love, and they can teach us some of life's greatest lessons. To all the Grandparents that don't hear it enough...we love you! And to mine- Thank you.

To the wonderful friends who brought us new memories and much laughter on Sanibel Island, thank you! Sharing that piece of paradise with us has brought more joy to our souls. We love you like family, and look forward to many more bike rides, and long beach days. Some places are put into your life for a reason, and I am most certain that Island has been one of them.

Written "In Loving Memory" of Granny and
Mamaw Cheeseburger.

Letters from Nan

Some call it hope or fate, I call it love.

Past...

Standing out on the beach holding my water pale and shovel, I watch the waves crash into the shore. The vibrant blue ocean glistens as the sun sparkles on the water, and the sounds of the waves roll back out into the sea.

Looking around, I rush towards any shells that float up in my direction, missing most of them, only to leave sand in my empty hands. Stomping my foot in frustration, I toss my bucket over my head only to hear a loud yelp from a boy's voice. Startled by the voice, I jump and spin around to see him holding my bucket in his hands, the shovel lies on the ground beside his feet.

"Lucas, I am so sorry," I said, feeling guilty. Walking closer to me, he asks in an angry tone, "What did you do that for?" Huffing out a breath, I answer, "I can't grab these shells that are washing up on the beach! So, I'm done with that bucket and shovel. You can have them, I don't want them anymore."

Looking out at the water, he asks, "Why do you want a shell anyways?" "Because they are beautiful," I reply with narrowed eyes. He laughs and mutters, "Must be a silly girl thing." Angry, I put my hands on my hips, tilting my head to the side, asking in a snarky tone, "Are you going to help me, or not?" "Alright, I will," he replied as he rolled his eyes.

Hours went by that day, and when we made it back to the beach house with more shells than we knew what to do with, we were thrilled. Telling anyone and everyone we could find all about the shells, and how many we had found. We were just two small kids without a care in the world that quickly became best friends.

A few years went by and our friendship only grew stronger. When we weren't racing to the beach to hunt for seashells, we were building sandcastles, or helping Nan bake cookies, while eating most of the dough ourselves. We had this connection that not many young people had, and while we were young and unaware of it, we treasured our friendship.

There were times when we fought, but times that we laughed together so hard our bellies hurt. Lucas always had that big brother persona when he was around me. He acted as if he were always watching over me, and it was his job in keeping me safe.

I remember a summer when Lucas and I had stayed out on the beach all day. His brothers had some friends come along with them that trip, which kept them occupied most days and away from us. Lucas never brought anyone, it was always just he and I for the summers.

We were walking back up from the water when I was abruptly knocked over by what felt like a brick wall. Lucas had just said something that made me laugh, and while I was only paying attention to him, I saw his face instantly morph into worry as he tried to push by me. He wasn't quick enough though, and a jolt to my head sent me rolling in the sand.

Opening my eyes, I saw Lucas leaning down over me, asking if I was alright? His brothers and their friends stood behind him, one was holding a Frisbee. Trying to shake off the pain in my head, I saw the furry in Lucas's eyes. One of the friends said with a chuckle, "Dang, she took that like a champ!" I just knew as soon as the words left his mouth there was going to be trouble.

Even though we were only in middle school, and they were in High School, Lucas never seemed to back down to anyone, especially if it meant protecting me. He lunged at the boy, both jolting down from the hit to the sand. As his brothers pulled him off, both of them yelling at him as he got in another punch, I screamed his name. Everyone just froze. Lucas's eyes were dark with anger as his brothers shook their heads at one another. Their friend stood up and brushed the sand off of him, cursing back at Lucas.

Lucas finally shook their hands off his shoulders while cursing under his break, then walked back over to me and helped me up. Grabbing me by the elbow, he walked us back to the beach house. I remember walking through the sand as they all yelled over our shoulders at Lucas, but he only had one care in the world--me.

More time went by, and as our friendship grew, so did we. From young kids on the beach to teenagers flying kites and eating ice cream at the Diner. Lucas and I had grown up together. Our parents were best friends and both had vacation homes on beautiful Sanibel Island which we visited every Spring Break, Summer, and any other reason they could come up with.

We all not only came as just a family, but through the years had brought friends and extended family with us, mixing our two-family circles more and more. No matter who came with the two families, Lucas and I were never far apart from one another. It seemed like we were always looking for another reason to go see the other.

Over the years our families meshed together as if we were one big happy family that just kept on growing. From early mornings to late nights, we would all be together whether it was sitting out on the beach, playing in the ocean, riding bikes, or grilling out.

The houses both sat side by side on the beach, allowing both sets of growing families plenty of room. Both had a huge wrap-around porch on the backside that overlooked the ocean. They were so close you could throw a football back and forth from one to the other, which often the boys did. Many times they had hit a window or knocked over glasses, which eventually led to footballs being prohibited on the decks.

I was an only child with one of the sweetest mothers, whom everyone adored. My father on the other hand, was the funny guy of the group. He was constantly pulling pranks, and making people laugh. Their personalities were welcoming to anyone. My parents were high school sweethearts, and had been happily married since College. My dad treated my mom like she walked on water, constantly flocking to her every need, and treating her like the Queen she truly was. Their love for each other was like no other.

I was always catching them hugging or kissing in a room. One time Lucas and I walked home after school one day, and as we walked into our Kitchen we both made a vomit noise in disgust as we watched them kiss passionately, sparkles in my mother's eyes. They both laughed as my father dipped my mother back, making her laugh even harder. I always acted as if it bothered me, but deep down, I was just glad they were so happy.

My Nan, whose name was Ida, always came on our vacations, too. She was the baker of the family, always putting out the best smells throughout the house, which was the main cause of all the children constantly coming over. They all wanted her sweet treats. My Nan was my father's mother. Nan was the type of person that you could confide in about anything. She made me feel better when I was sick but always knew how to make me laugh. There is something about a Grandmother's hug that just instantly makes everything so much better.

Lucas was the youngest of three boys. His parents were both in real estate, so planning trips with our family was easy because they set their own schedules. They too had met in High School but had not gotten together until after College. Lucas's dad always joked that he liked the chase, while his mother would just smile and shake her head.

The two sets of parents had all gone to high school together, growing up best friends, and then raising their families together. Our lives were like a perfect story with a little bit of chaos mixed in.

Chapter 1

Spreading my blanket out on the sand, I took in everything. The sun was blistering hot today, but there was just enough of a breeze to cool you down. The ocean water looked clear and crisp, while the sounds of birds hummed in the distance. Taking a deep breath and closing my eyes, I took in the smell of the salty air and felt my body relax.

Rubbing in the last of my sunscreen, I wiped my hands off on my towel, laying down on it with my book in hand. Taking a deep breath, I smiled to myself knowing that this was the start of summer, and we would be here for most of it. This was the one place I came to that I felt like myself. I felt strong, safe, and well, I just loved it here.

Brushing some sand off of my blanket, I had just opened my book when I heard his voice. "Watch out!" Rolling over, I looked up as it all happened so fast. "Ouch!" I groaned as Lucas landed on me. Trying to catch his body from crushing mine, he rolled over me, but managed to get tangled up in my legs, taking me with him as we rolled off the towel and into the sand.

Feeling a jolt to my head, I realized he had elbowed me in the forehead. "Lucas!" I screamed.

Laughing, he looked down at me but still didn't move. He was practically straddling me with both forearms locked in the sand around my head. "Get off of me!" I yelled, pushing at his hard chest. Still laughing, he rolled off as he helped me up.

I tried brushing the sand off my hot, now sweaty skin, noticing that my book was laying on the ground next to a football, while my blanket was covered in sand at our feet. Laughter erupted from down the beach as I saw Lucas's two older brothers jogging our way.

"Jayda, are you okay?" he asked, still chuckling to himself. "Are you kidding me? You just jumped right on top of me." I replied, fuming at the smirk he was trying to hide. "I didn't jump on you," he replied sarcastically. "I gently fell on you," he said with a smile. "Lucas, it's not funny. I think you gave me a concussion," I yelled, as I rubbed my head. "Don't exaggerate Jayda, you are fine," he barked back, as he tussled my hair with his hands.

Moving out from under his hand I groaned, "Don't! You are getting sand in my hair with your grimy fingers." Laughing, he tilted his head and replied as his eyes roamed up and down my body, "I think the sand was already there." I don't think my glare could have been any more intense at his remark. Annoyed at his comment, I sighed loudly as my jaw clenched.

His brothers were both now standing next to us with cheese grins plastered on their faces. John, his older brother, asked if I was alright as Brayden picked up the football and pitched it lightly to John. "Whatever, I'm fine," I say to them all, turning back around towards my things. "Jayda, don't get so worked up," Lucas says over my shoulder as I grab my stuff up off the sand.

"I'll help you back to the house," Brayden offers, reaching for my things. Lucas glares at him, grabbing my bag out of his brother's hands. "I'll take her," Lucas awkwardly replies. Both his brothers share a look and then back to Lucas with a coy grin.

Glaring at him, I roll my eyes and grab my bag back out of his hands. "I can walk myself," I say sharply, heading for the house. "Come on Jayda, stay out! You just got out here, and now you are going back inside?" he groans. I stop dead in my tracks and turn around. "Why, so you can run over me some more?" I question.

He crosses his arms and tilts his head at me. "Come on, it was an accident," he mutters softly while giving me those puppy dog eyes he knows I fall for every time. "Dang it, Lucas!" I scold. "Ha! You can't be mad at me," he says, laughing and taking a small step towards me. I narrow my eyes at him, knowing that the look on his face means trouble.

He begins to run at me as I quickly take a few steps backward. Wrapping his arms around my waist, knocking everything from my hands, he begins to carry me to the water. Screaming, I yell, "Lucas! Lucas put me down!" Looking over my shoulder, I see both of our parents watching from the deck, just shaking their heads, while his two brothers are already walking down the beach towards a few other girls.

Wiggling in his arms, I try to free myself from under his grasp, but he holds me tight. Whispering in my ear, he says, "Don't pry or I'll toss you in the water, Jayda." Smiling at me, he laughs again, only this time he boasts a mischievous look in his eyes. "You wouldn't dare?" I murmur, giving him a death stare over my shoulder as we wade out into the ocean.

Waves hit our legs, and soon begin to reach my stomach. "Lucas! Stop!" I yell again, followed by a chuckle. Feeling the coolness brush against my skin, I tense at not only the touch of the salty water but Lucas's strong hands gripping my hips firmly.

Finally, he stops and lowers me down his body, still holding onto me as we both face the waves crashing in. Twisting in his arms, I try to squirm away from his grip, but he just chuckles and twists me back around. Now, we are shoulder-deep in the water, and my back is pressing against his slippery, tight, muscular chest. I can feel his breathing in my ear as he leans his head down closer to my cheek.

His grip loosens a bit as our bodies take to the water, beginning to float a little more, but he never lets me go. His hands press against my skin, making a shiver roll through me. Gently whispering in my ear, I hear him ask, "You okay?" Taking a deep breath as a wave comes towards us, I close my mouth, turning my face closer to his. His grip losens just a bit as I feel him spin me around. I turn into him, wrapping my arms around his neck as we gaze back at one another.

Lucas drops his hands from my hips and tries to pull my legs around him, allowing the water to hold most of our weight. We are so close now that I can feel the beating of his chest against mine, as my heart pounds with a newfound desire. As we break the top of the wave together, water droplets drip from his nose as I wipe my eyes and face.

This wasn't the first time he had drug me out into the water, but it was the first time I felt butterflies in my stomach at his touch on my skin. For a brief second, I could see a hint of lust in his smoky eyes as he stared back at me. That look he gave me seemed heated, but it quickly faded back to his playfulness as he pulled me in tighter to his body. It wasn't the first wave we needed to worry about though, it was the next.

The wave knocked both of us from one another. Coming up for air, I gasp as I wipe my eyes. Looking around, I can't find Lucas. "Lucas!" I yell. "Lucas! I yell again. Beginning to completely freak out, I dive under the water, coming up to nothing. I dive down again, only this time when I come up I see Lucas, smiling as he floats in the water. "Lucas! I yelled again, reaching for him. "Are you okay? I couldn't find you."

Smirking, he replied, "Yeah, I know. I was just playing with you." Glaring at him, I smacked the water with my hand in his direction. "Not funny. Not funny at all. I was freaking out!" I yelled at him as I began to swim away.

Gripping my arm, he pulled me back closer to him, looking at me with those playful eyes. "Let go," I say bluntly. "Jayda, come on, I'm sorry. I was just playing with you." Frustrated I reply, "Yeah, you are good at that today, aren't you? Just leave me alone, Lucas." Letting go of my arm, he shouts, "Whatever Jayda, you just need to chill out sometimes." Turning around and looking at him, I say nothing and swim away.

Walking up the steps to the house I hear our parents inside playing cards. Nan is sitting on her swing on the deck looking out over the beach. "Everything alright, dear?" she asks me. "Yeah, just great," I replied. "Looks like you forgot something out there, or should I say, someone," she says with a smile.

Looking back to the water I see Lucas, still out in the water, floating around. Rolling my eyes again, I mutter, "He can stay out there for good for all I care." Nan chuckles and says, "You would be lost without that boy, sweetie." Sitting down next to her, I laugh. "Nan, I don't think so. Lucas has changed as we have gotten older. He's too arrogant, and doesn't think before he does anything," I reply.

Nan takes a deep breath before speaking, "Your Grandfather drove me crazy when we were younger. Do you want to know what I loved most about him?" Looking to her for an answer, I ask, "What?" "Just that, dear. I loved that he could keep me on my toes constantly, and I loved that he made me feel like I was his entire world." Smiling at her, I sighed, looking back out to the water at Lucas, who was now swimming into the shore.

"That boy out there," her gaze traveling to Lucas, "His world is you, and it has been for many years. You two have so much ahead of you, and you don't even know it yet," she says. Looking back to the beach, I see Lucas staring up at my house as he heads towards his parent's place. Laughing at her words, I stand up, grabbing my bag. "Nan, I love you, but you are crazy sometimes." Nan just smiles and pats my back as I walk inside.

Chapter 2

After Dinner, Jayda disappeared out to the beach to walk along the shore. Sitting down, she thought back to what Nan had said. "His world is you." Jayda had never thought about Lucas like that before. Well, maybe a little, but they were always such good friends that she didn't think he felt like that way about her. Over the years she may have noticed his looks more, and that smile drove her insane. But, he was her best friend and she never wanted to lose that.

When they were kids they just played, but as they had gotten older things had changed. Even though she didn't want to admit it to herself, Lucas looked at her differently, and she noticed him more often than she should. Lucas had a way of making her feel so safe and full of life. Over the years, Lucas had changed from a boy to a man, and it was noticed by many. His charm was given out to everyone, but his smile, she wanted all for herself.

"Is this seat taken?" a timid, gruff voice behind her asked. Looking up she saw Lucas. Smirking, she replied, "Yes, it is actually." Surprised by her answer, he chuckled slowly, "Okay." He began to turn around, but Jayda caught the bottom of his shorts, tugging at them. Looking at her, he paused. "I'm saving it for my best friend," she said with a wink. Smiling, he sat down next to her, wrapping his arm around her shoulders.

"Jayda, I'm sorry about today. I pushed you too far," he said. "It's fine. I should not have gotten so mad and worked up," she replied. The two just stared at one another as the waves hit the shore. The cool evening air blew by them causing Jayda to shiver and pull her sleeves down to her wrists.

Lucas pulled her closer to him as she leaned into his arms. Speaking softly, Lucas asked, "Forgive me?" "Lucas, I don't think I could stay mad at you even if I wanted to," she replied. Grinning, he pulled her to him and kissed her forehead. Lowering her head to his shoulder, she looked out into the sea.

"Lucas, today when I couldn't find you out in the water, I was so scared," Jayda finally said, looking up at him. Lucas frowned, "I told you, I took it too far, I know I should not have done that." Turning to him, her expression filled with sadness. "No, like I freaked out. For a split second, I thought I had lost you, and I totally freaked out," she admitted quietly.

Furrowing his brows, confused at what she was saying he asked, "Why did you freak out so bad?" With a hint of embarrassment and pink-tinted cheeks, she replied, "I guess I just don't want to lose you. When I came up and you weren't there, I didn't know what to do. You are always there, but then you weren't."

Keeping his arm around her shoulder, he moved his other hand to interlock his fingers with hers. Jayda's eyes moved up from their hands on her lap to see Lucas's smoky eyes staring back at her with lust. "Jayda, you will never lose me," he admits softly.

Dropping her hand, he places his palm on her cheek, rubbing his thumb down her jawline. Their lips are inches apart, and his hand is still on her cheek as the breeze blows a few hairs across her face. Looking to her lips, Lucas tries to steady his breathing, unable to look away from her. As Jayda bites down on her lip, flustered at their interaction, she feels Lucas moving in closer.

Voices from down the beach break their gazes as Lucas's two brothers yell, "You two joining us tonight at the Bon Fire? Should be a lot of fun," Brayden adds. Dropping his hand from her cheek, Lucas stands up quickly, rubbing his hand across his face.

Taking a deep breath, he looks a little annoyed as he holds out his hand to help her up. He asks, "Do you want to go?" "Sure, I guess so," Jayda replies. Pausing for a moment with her hand in his, he looks to her as if he wants to say something, but instead, drops her hand and heads towards his brothers.

Bonfires on the beach were normal for private beaches. Jayda's parents had a fire pit they set out on the beach at night; there is something about roasting a marshmallow on the beach that makes it so much better. One of Jayda's favorite things to do was to sit out by the fire at night and listen to the ocean waves ripple in. The night breeze on the beach usually was a little chilly so the fire was a nice way to warm up and still stay outside.

Watching the stars in the sky and listening to the waves was so peaceful. One of Jayda's favorite childhood memories was of Lucas and his brothers making s'mores with her, and eventually eating more sand than chocolate just because they dropped the s'mores so many times on the beach.

It was the last summer before Jayda and Lucas were seniors in High School and they both knew that the next few years were going to be different as they prepared to leave for College. They had talked about trying to get back to the beach during those summers while they were at school, but neither really knew if that would happen for a while.

They attended the same High School and were inseparable. Best friends and rarely apart. People often at times assumed they were dating, but they never were. When people asked, they just shrugged it off with laughter. They were best friends, that was all.

Jayda had tried to date a few guys, all of which Lucas didn't like. They would go out a few times and eventually she would have to pick between the relationships or her friendship--she always chose Lucas.

The two had chosen different Colleges so the thought of being apart was hard, but they told themselves they would talk constantly and have other friends to keep them occupied while gone. Lucas had wanted to follow Jayda to College more than anything. When he didn't get accepted, he didn't have the strength to tell her the honest truth so he lied and said it was because he wanted to go somewhere else.

Jayda was so upset that night. She came straight home after he had told her and cried her eyes out. She couldn't talk to anyone about it because she knew they would think it was because she had feelings for him. Her heart ached for him, and while he was her best friend, she didn't want to do anything to mess that up. She just assumed that his feelings were pure friendship rather he would have gone with her.

Lucas knew if he told Jayda that he had not been accepted she would change her plans and go where he went. The last few months had been hard for both of them, secretly. Always trying to shake off their feelings for one another, but now it got harder. Neither knew how the other truly felt.

Almost back to the beach house from the bonfire, Lucas stopped just past the dunes. "Lucas, what are you doing?" Jayda asked, looking back at him as he stood just a few feet away. Turning towards the water putting his hands on his neck he sighed, "Jayda, I need to tell you something. I should have told you a long time ago, and I don't know why I waited, but I can't wait any longer."

Confused, Jayda began to walk back towards him and asked, "What's wrong?" Lucas quickly grabbed her arm and pulled her farther behind a dune. "Lucas, what on earth are you doing," she questioned. "I'm not really sure," he said with a nervous smile. "I do know I have wanted to do this for years though." Still confused, Jayda asked, "Do what?"

Stepping in closer he cupped her face in his hands, gently pulling her into his chest. Now, his lips were mere inches from hers as he searched her eyes for any anger or worry. His chest was beating heavy, and the need he had for her pushed him over the edge for more. Finally, he covered his mouth with hers and kissed her so sweetly he felt her body relax a bit in his arms. The touch was pure bliss.

When Jayda pulled back from him he thought she was mad, but instead, she gave him the biggest smile and jumped back into his arms. Losing his balance, Jayda fell on top of Lucas, the two just laying there, laughing on the sand as the waves crashed to the shore.

Rolling over, Lucas brushed the sand off her cheek as she ran her hands through his hair. "What are we doing?" she asked him softly. "What we should have done a long time ago," he answered. Their breaths turned erratic as their thoughts ran wild, and emotions tugged at them full force.

Their lips met again, only this time with an intensity neither could deny. They stayed out there for what seemed like hours, caught up in each other, unable to deny their attraction, and only wanting more.

Chapter 3

They had been sneaking around together the last two weeks, finding every chance to meet where no one else was. Summer was winding down, and they had their last days ahead of them.

Jayda was crazy about Lucas, and he felt the same about her. Over the years their friendship had always been strong and full of love, but now it seemed those emotions had taken the sparks of friendship to a whole new meaning.

The two wandered up the back deck holding hands, gazing at one another, in awe at how their newly found desires had consumed them the last few weeks. When they reached the top, Lucas gently pulled Jayda towards him as he looked next door to see their families all inside his house. He could see them, but their view was not as good.

Smiling to her, Lucas pulled Jayda in close, gently rubbing her cheek with one hand as he backed her up to the deck rail. Trailing his hands down her back, just about to kiss her when they heard a throat clear.

"Nan!" Jayda gasped, her eyes going wide. "Hello, dear," Nan answered with a grin. "And what are you two up to this evening?" Nan asked them with curiosity laced in her tone.

Embarrassed, Jayda fumbles her words, dropping his hand, while Lucas just grins at Nan. "Sorry Nan," he replies, filled with mischief. "For what dear?" she asks him, standing up, and heading for the door. Jayda rubs her fingers on her temple trying to decide what to say.

"Both of you be sure to shake that sand off of your clothes before you come in this house, you hear?" she says sarcastically, walking through the door. Jayda's mouth drops open as Lucas laughs and rubs the back of his neck, a little shocked at Nan's jab. "She is a ball of fire, isn't she?" he says.

Looking to Lucas, Jayda just smiles, slapping him on the chest, "Yes, she is!" Lucas snatches her hand and pulls her to him, fiercely kissing her. Walking back down the steps, the two join their families next door knowing Nan won't say anything to anyone.

A noise wakes Jayda from her sleep. Looking up she reads the clock on her phone, 2:30 am. Wiping the sleep from her eyes, she sits up and listens. She hears the noise again, only this time she realizes it's coming from her window. Walking over to peer out, she sees Lucas, looking up at her from the top deck with a heated grin.

Opening the window, Jayda hisses, "Lucas, what are you doing?" "Come down here," he says. "No!" she replies with a laugh. "If dad catches you out here, he is going to strangle you. First, he is going to ask what the heck you are doing, and then he is going to pass out when he finds out we are together."

Again, smiling at her words, he says, "You have to come down, I need to tell you something." Groaning she replies, "Can it wait until morning?" "Jayda if you don't come down here right now, I'm going to profess my feelings for you right here on this deck for everyone to hear. I don't care if they hear me or not," he responds, grinning, but raising his voice a little louder.

Chuckling to herself, Jayda shakes her head knowing he really would do it. "Be quiet, I'm coming down," she whispers. "Jayda, jump from there, I'll catch you," he says with a smirk. Rolling her eyes, she closes the window and tosses on some clothes.

Walking outside the breeze is light, but chilly. "I can't believe I'm out here right now," she says. "Someone is going to wake up, Nan already busted us tonight once." "Nan doesn't care," Lucas said. "She has known about us for a while now, it is obvious." Tilting her head at him, grinning wildly with pink-tinted cheeks she replies, "Oh great!"

Wrapping her in his arms, he pulls her towards the swing on the deck. "You are crazy," she chuckles. "That's nothing new, babe," he answers. "How long have we known each other, and you are just realizing this?" he asks. "No, I knew it from day one," she said sheepishly. Grinning, he leans into her and kisses her sweetly.

"Jayda, I need to tell you something," he admits. "Okay," she replies slowly, pulling him in closer for another kiss. "I can't sleep," he says. Gasping, she rolls her eyes. "Please tell me that's not why you woke me up," she asks, punching his arm. "No," he chuckles. "I couldn't sleep because all I could think about was you." Her cheeks were rosy now, her smile full of emotion and desire for him. "Lucas," she questions softly. "Jayda, you are my best friend, and I-- I love you," he says.

Looking into his eyes, she sees that while Lucas constantly teases and jokes with her, this time his words meant so much more. Hesitating only for a few seconds, allowing what he said to sink in, she pulls him to her for a kiss. Pulling back, he says again, "Jayda, I love you." Placing her soft hand on his cheek she smiles at him as she replies, Lucas, I love you."

Beaming, he pulls her up and into his arms. Spinning her around, his smile so contagious that she can't stop grinning. Picking her up, he wraps her legs around his waist and carries her down the steps to the beach fully intending on showing her how deep his love for her is.

Hours go by, and the two are walking back towards the house as the sun is beginning to rise. Lucas has Jayda tucked into his arm, stopping every few feet to kiss her cheek, lips, neck. Giggles come from Jayda as his breaths on her soft skin fill her with lust.

Unable to get enough of each other, Lucas spins her around to him and wraps his arms tightly around her. "I love you so much, I'm just sorry it took this long to tell you," he says. Gripping his shirt with one hand as the other moves down his chest Jayda smiles into their kiss. "I love you, Lucas- so much," she replies with a sparkle in her eyes.

Walking backward, still wrapped up in one another, Lucas buries his nose in her neck, gently kissing a trail to her mouth. "Lucas, we really need to get back," Jayda says. "I know," he responds, but not wanting the night to end.

As the two get closer to the houses, their emotions are caught off guard by the commotion at Jayda's. Looking at each other with panic, they begin to full-on sprint when they see flashing lights. Running up the back steps Nan is sitting on the swing, sobbing. Looking up she sees Jayda and begins to sob even harder. "Nan, what's going on?" she asks in heavy breaths.

Just then, Lucas's mom and dad walk through the door, sorrow in their bloodshot eyes as Jayda's dad is behind them on the floor with his hands in his hair, sobbing hysterically. Jayda looks to Lucas with horror in her eyes as she runs to her father. Their night had been about love, but what they didn't know was love was breakable, and the worst had just shattered it all.

Chapter 4

Do you ever ask yourself why bad things happen to good people? How can a person who is smart, loving, and kind have their life completely flipped inside out?

Guilt floods Jayda and seems to just keep piling up. A tear falls down her cheek as she watches the sea. Sitting on the beach, looking out onto the water, she closes her eyes, just allowing the light sea breeze to blow through her hair. Sucking in a breath she wipes her tears and pulls her legs in closer to her chest.

Startled by movement, she turns around. "Lucas, you scared the crap out of me," she said, faintly. Hesitant, he stops, pondering whether he should keep moving forward. Looking at her he asks, "Can I sit?" Not answering him, she just turns back to the waves looking drained. Lucas settles on the sand next to her. Pain seeps into her heart, filling as if it is broken. Which in fact, it is.

I'm not going to ask you if you are okay because I know you are not. I just want you to know that I am here for you whenever you need me. Day or night,

Jayda, I'm here," he chokes out in a hoarse voice. Another tear drips down her face as she rests her chin on her knees. "Thanks, Lucas," is all she could say.

Sliding right next to her, he wraps his arms around her, pulling her closer to him. Feeling at ease in his arms, she rests her head on his chest and begins to cry.

The next few days were all just a blur. Arrangements being made, people crying, and everyone asking her how she was doing. How did they think she was doing? Running down the steps, barely able to catch her breath, she snuck into the back room, closing the door behind her.

Sinking down the wall, she leaned her head back against it and began to sob. Crying is all she seemed to do the last few days, it's all she could do. She couldn't speak to anyone and kept hoping she would wake up and it would all just be a bad dream.

"Hearing her name being called, she held her breath, hoping they would pass by and not follow her. Footsteps paused at the door, just before she heard the knob creak as it was turned. She cringed when it slowly opened, but breathed a sigh of relief when he walked in. Closing the door behind him, he slid down next to Jayda and grabbed her hand. "What can I do? Jayda, just tell me and I will do it, please." he pleaded.

Looking at her, he noticed dark circles around her eyes and the ominous tone of her skin. Reaching up, he wiped a tear away with his finger that was gliding down her cheek as she answered with one word, "You." Pulling her tightly into his chest, he held her as he rubbed her back, lost in his own guilt. This time she didn't cry harder, she just felt safe, as if she weren't even there anymore, living out this terrible dream."

Kissing the top of her head he told her, I'm so sorry, Jayda. I'm so sorry about your mom. Just saying the words hurt. His stomach ached, and his gut swirled. He knew his Jayda was lost, and even he couldn't bring her back. He had always been there for her, but this time was different because he didn't know if he was truly what she needed.

Jayda and her mother had been extremely close. Being an only child, and her father traveling a lot for work, left the two at home alone many nights. Movie nights and dinner dates were always on their calendar.

After her mother began to work again, Nan had moved into the home. Most nights the three would spend time baking in the kitchen, or watching any chick flick they could find while eating Nan's homemade caramel-cooked popcorn.

Her mother was a delight. She was so full of life, and always made Jayda feel as if she could do anything in the world. Oftentimes, Jayda found herself staring at her mother in awe at how great she truly was.

The Doctor told them it was a massive stroke--a ruptured aneurysm. Nothing they could have done differently could have saved her, but Jayda didn't believe that. She had thought if she just would have been there, maybe there was something she could have done differently.

Her mother had been complaining of migraines lately, but nothing out of the normal. She had those often, and had since Jayda was in middle school. Her mother always said it was nothing, and brushed it off.

That night at the beach house, having to watch her father sob while sitting on the floor was miserable. Running to him and screaming for her mother, the thoughts haunted her dreams every night.

The hardest part for her was that she wasn't even there to say goodbye. She had snuck out with Lucas, and while her family needed her, she was gone.

Chapter 5

Months had gone by, and Lucas had tried everything. Since that night at the beach, things had been different. Since that moment at the funeral when he held her in his arms, things had been different. Jayda had changed into someone he didn't even recognize anymore. The girl he fell in love with was gone, and now, this new Jayda only tried to push him further away.

"Jayda, hey! How are your classes going?" Lucas asked her as he walked up to her locker in the hall. Looking up to him with a blank stare, she replied, "They are fine." Setting her books inside the locker, she closed the door quickly and started to walk away. "Jayda!" Lucas said loudly.

Looking at him over one shoulder, he looked so lost. "Jayda, talk to me, please. I told you, I am so sorry." Turning back around, she muttered, "I have to go, sorry." Standing there in the hallway, Lucas felt a hole in his stomach. All the years they had been friends, and the time he knew she needed him the most, she just pushed him away more and more. Sorrow filled her beautiful eyes, and it was all he could do to watch her walk away.

Walking up to her door, he knocked for what seemed like the first time in years. When they were younger, he would sometimes even just walk in the back door, announcing he was there. But, that was when things were different. When Jayda's mother would greet him in the kitchen, or see him coming and yell for Jayda to come down. Always had a smile on her face when she would see Lucas.

Thinking back to not only her kindness but her mother's beauty inside and out made him smile to himself. He missed her so much, and so did everyone else.

Jayda's father had not only lost a wife that night, but he had found out that Jayda and Lucas had been sneaking around together. While he mourned the loss of his wife, he seemed to take some of the anger out on Lucas for the deceit, which put a tight grudge between the families.

His parents were there through everything during the funeral, but since, they had kept their distance. Jayda's father, like Jayda, pushed everyone he loved away, especially Lucas and his family. Her father was no longer the fun guy, he too had changed.

The door opened and Nan greeted him. Nan was always a breath of fresh air, but even she had changed a little. "Lucas, how are you dear?" she asked. "I'm doing okay, Nan, thanks. How are you?" he replied. "Every day is a new day, so just trying to get by," she said with sadness in her tone.

"Is Jayda home?" he asked her. Looking down at the floor and then back to him, she sighed. "Honey, she is, but she's not up for talking this afternoon. Maybe just give her time, Lucas," she replied to him. Defeated, he answered, "Thanks, Nan," and walked away.

This went on for months. Jayda ignoring him, or just barely speaking in passing when they saw each other. She no longer went out with friends, and her family no longer joined Lucas's for Sunday dinners. Since her mother's death, the two families seemed as if they never even coexisted.

Graduation was here, and while families stood around beaming with joy, snapping pictures, Nan could barely get Jayda and her father to take a single one. The thought of her mother not being here was too hurtful, and the memories swarmed back around.

"Jayda!" a voice yelled over the crowd, as Lucas and his family approached them. His brothers had made it home for graduation, and while they looked much older, they were still the young boys she grew up with on the beach.

Nodding to his family with a slight grin, her father said Congratulations as Lucas got closer. Being the first nice thing he had said in months, caught Lucas off guard. Their last conversation had ended with yelling, and her father telling Lucas to stay away from them.

Stopping in front of Jayda, Lucas smiled, "Hey!" he said softly. Her distant look made him miserable, and his heart ached for her smile again. Months of regret and longing stood in between them now, and he didn't know how to fix it.

Their parents mingled a bit, catching up on the last few months, seeming to only chat about the weather and gossip around town. Their friendship too, lost in sorrow.

Looking at him, Jayda's heart felt like it could burst. She had not meant to push him so far away this year, but deep down she did feel guilty for her mother's death. A small part, just a very small part, she blamed on Lucas, too. If he had not taken her from her home that night, maybe she could have been there for her mother.

Sensing her hesitation, Lucas asked, "Will you take a picture with me?" looking to Nan who held the camera. Looking back to him and then to Nan, Jayda nodded, "Sure." Lucas leaned into Jayda, wrapping his arm around her as the two stood still for the camera.

Jayda didn't show much happiness, but Lucas didn't care as long as he had her near him. Nan grinned and snapped the photo. The two stood there looking at one another, lost in the possibilities of their relationship.

Last summer, their dreams, and love had been about one another, and now it was all gone. While they both had an empty soul, their thoughts were still running wild about each other. Blinking her eyes, Jayda turned her head back down to the ground, breaking his gaze from her.

"Good Luck at College, Lucas," Jayda muttered, sadness laced in her voice. His heartfelt like it could burst, just seeing how empty she was. He knew deep down she needed time, but even then, so much sadness circled their memories that even he didn't know if that would help.

He wanted to pick her up and make everything go back to how it was before her mother's death. He wanted the old Jayda back, and to tell her how much he still loved her. He wanted to grab her by the shoulders and kiss her like never before. But, he couldn't. He could not do any of it, because she was no longer his

Jayda. Lucas grinned at her and responded, "Thanks Jayda, you too."

As the two families walked away from each other, Jayda looked back over her shoulder to see Lucas staring at her. His eyes lost for her, and her soul crushed. The love of her life, she was leaving behind, and her mother was gone forever.

Unsure of how she was going to balance life with so much loss, she dropped her head as Nan wrapped her up in a hug.

Chapter 6

1 year later...

"Dad, I have been at College for a year now, I think I know how to stay safe," I say through the phone. "I know. Yes, I know," I assured him. "Yes, dad. I have the pepper spray and I know how to still use it," rolling my eyes at his crazy questioning. "Tell Nan I love her. Bye, love you too, Dad."

Hanging up the phone, I look at my roommate and toss the phone on my bed. "Can you believe he wants me to actually spray it to see if it still works? He's crazy, I swear it," I say, groaning, plopping back down on my bed with a thud.

Laughter from across the room echoes off the walls as Becca rolls her eyes, and continues hanging her clothes in the closet. "He's just worried," she says, still giggling. "Just lie to him and tell him you tested the pepper spray and it works fine," she replies, placing one hand on her hip, smiling back at me.

Sitting upright on my bed, I glare at Becca. "He wants you to video it," I say, raising my eyebrows drastically at her. "Okay, now he is crazy!" Becca responds, placing the palm of her hand across her forehead, and blowing out a deep breath.

Becca and I met a few months after my first year of college. I had kept to myself mostly, but Becca was in a few of my classes, and when we got paired up for a Physics class assignment we just began to hit it off.

I poured my heart out one night to her about my mother, even telling her about Lucas. Becca had leaned in and hugged me as the tears streamed down my face. That night I knew she and I would become great friends.

While I missed Lucas so much and had even begun to dial his number a few times, I thought it was best to move on, and leave that part of my life in the past. Besides, it wasn't like he had reached out lately. He had probably moved on too.

"Are you planning on unpacking all of this tonight?" Becca asked. "Because you are going to a party with me!" she exclaimed loudly, as she clapped her hands several times.

We had just returned to school for a new year, and while I stayed at home with Nan and my father, Lucas's family had decided to stay at their beach house in Sanibel the entire summer.

Not having seen each other at all, made the thoughts of what he was doing wandering around in my mind often these last few weeks. I missed him so much, but time and pain had separated us.

Becca and I had gotten a small apartment together, and while my father was not loving the idea of his only daughter being three hours away at school, he was glad that I had made a new friend. He seemed to like Becca and had even mentioned a time or two that he felt she was good for me.

Shrugging my shoulders at Becca, I grimaced and narrowed my eyes at her, answering, "I don't know if I'm up for anything tonight." Becca dropped the top she was holding to the floor and just stared at me sternly.

"You are going. End of story," she said, placing her hand on her hip again and smiling. "Becca," I groaned. "Why are you trying to make me live this full College dream?" I teasingly asked in a peppy tone. "Because, last year we didn't do much, and I let you have your time and space. But, this year, we are going all out!" Becca said with enthusiasm, as she threw her hands up in the air.

Laughing at her, I smiled and knew that Becca was just the friend I needed to move forward this year. Her friend had given me a new beginning, and I needed to start taking advantage of it before it was too late.

Walking into the frat house, Becca smiled at me. "See, doesn't this look fun?" she asked. Looking around at beer cans and red solo cups on the floor as music blasted from a radio on a ping pong table, I replied unenthusiastically, "Sure, tons of fun!" Rolling her eyes at me, she replied, full of sarcasm, "Can you just try to enjoy yourself, please?"

We had been at the party only about an hour when we heard loud noises from the backyard. Chants and cheering got louder, and of course, Becca got curious. Walking towards the back door I followed Becca as she led the way.

As we approached the group of people scattered outside, Becca asked, "Who is that good-looking guy?" Glancing in the direction she was starring, I saw a tall guy with messy blondish-brown hair. He was holding a beer bong for a group of girls while a group of guys cheered them on.

He was taller, with a muscular-athletic build, and broad shoulders. Throwing down the bong, the guy leaned down to kiss the girl on the cheek who had just drunk the beer. Laughter and chants erupted again as the next girl stepped up.

Looking at the guy, I quickly froze. My legs felt like jelly, and my stomach instantly felt hollow. "Oh my gosh!" I said out loud. "What?" Becca asked, walking down the stairs, while I stopped on the top step, looking out onto the yard.

"Let's do one!" Becca enthusiastically yelled. Still unable to say anything else, I stared at the guy who finally caught my gaze. He suddenly dropped the bong on the girl who was drinking the beer, spilling what was remaining all over her front side. The girl screamed, punching him in the arm, as the guys cheered louder now as the beer, which spilled all over her, clearly showed a definition of her white top.

The noise seemed to break the daze we were both stuck in as he looked down, quickly apologizing to the girl, as I stormed off through the door in the opposite direction.

Nearly down the sidewalk out front of the house, I felt a hand grab my wrist. "Jayda!" a masculine voice yelled. Knowing that voice by heart, I stopped with my eyes tightly closed, and turned around, opening them to find a very familiar face. "Hello, Lucas," I replied softly.

"Jayda, oh my gosh, it is so good to see you!" He said, leaning in for a hug. Awkwardly, hugging him, I leaned back from his touch. Narrowing his eyes with confusion, and tilting his head at me, he said sarcastically, "Wow, Lucas, it is so great to see you, too."

Rolling my eyes, I replied, "Why are you here, Lucas?" Stepping back, crossing his arms, he answered with a smirk, "I transferred." "You what?" I gasped loudly, surprised, and hoping he was joking. "I go here now," he answered proudly, still sporting the cocky grin. "Why?" I asked with a bit more attitude than an old friend deserved. "And how? Didn't you actually, not get accepted?" I asked sharply. He looked surprised that I knew, but almost regretting those words the second they left my mouth, I bit my bottom lip.

"How did you know that?" He asked, anger laced in his tone. "My dad might have mentioned it," I replied. "Of course he did," Lucas answered with a cold grimace. "What the heck does that mean?" I asked, in annoyance. "Nothing, nothing at all. I'm sure he will be thrilled I'm here though," Lucas replied.

Practically snarling at him now, anger in my eyes, but hurt more than anything that our first time seeing each other again was like this. Not in a million years did I think I would walk into that party and of all people, see Lucas.

"You better go back inside to your girlfriend," I say, nodding to the house. "She's not my girlfriend," he replied, with a smirk. "I don't have just one." My blood was now boiling as I looked at the boy I fell in love with just a few summers ago. He must have seen the hurt in my eyes at his sharp jab because his smirk fell quickly, and regret laced his face.

"Jayda, what are you doing?" Becca asked, briskly walking down the sidewalk towards us. As she approached and saw who I was talking to, she began to smile and greet Lucas saying, "Well, hello there." "Hey," Lucas said with a cheesy grin on his face.

"Becca, this is Lucas. Lucas, this is my roommate and best friend, Becca," I quickly introduced them. I see Becca's eyes go wide as she takes in who the hot guy is, and she then says, "So, this is Lucas? Wow! Jayda, you left out the hunk part of your story." "Story?" Lucas asks, raising his eyebrows at me. "We are leaving," I say abruptly, and begin to pull Becca's arm down the street.

Lucas
Watching her walk off like that, was brutal. He had purposely reapplied to the same College because he missed Jayda, so much. He had spoken to Nan a few times when he was home, and she had told him that Jayda wasn't doing well. She said that she knew deep down she missed him. Lucas had changed majors his

first year so it was easier to convince his parents that he should transfer schools for that reason. Getting good grades, and helping out in the study department had helped him get the transfer approved. Now, convincing Jayda to let him back in her life, was the next step.

Chapter 7

Having only one class together this semester, Jayda and Becca were both thankful it ended up being History class, because neither were too keen on the subject. The class was set up as a huge lecture hall that held about one hundred students.

Walking in and finding a seat near the back, I noticed Becca staring right at me with a smile that could kill. "Girl, don't look now, but a fine-looking man just walked in here," she said, raising her eyebrows with a goofy wiggle. Rolling my eyes, I looked up to see Lucas, and he was heading directly towards us. "You have got to be kidding me," I mumbled low under my breath.

Noticing an open seat next to us, I prayed someone else would quickly grab it. Looking to my left, I saw another guy smiling at me, briskly walking down the aisle towards the seat. Holding my breath and hoping he would get to it in time, I flinched when I caught the sight to my right.

Not my luck today, Lucas plopped down in the seat next to me with a huge grin plastered on his face.

Greeting Becca as he tossed his bag on the floor, and then glancing to me with a wink.

Looking grim, the other guy stopped in his tracks and spun around, grabbing a seat behind us that was open. Gritting my teeth, I rubbed my hand over my face, asking myself how this was all happening.

Lucas leaned into my personal space and spoke in a hushed whisper, so only I could hear, "Our first class together is History class? The irony, right?" he said with a light chuckle. Shooting him a cold look, I didn't reply as he winked at me. Tucking a strand of hair behind my ear, I sank down into my chair, praying this class would end early.

Leaving class, Becca and I were heading back towards our apartment when Lucas caught up to us. "Jayda!" he yelled, a little out of breath. "Can we talk?" "No!" I yelled sternly, not even stopping to look at him.

Laughing he said, "Boy nothing has changed. You are still stubborn, aren't you?" Stopping quickly, I spun around and replied, "No, I am not. I just have nothing to say to you." "There we go, I still know how to get you to speak to me," he chuckled with a wink.

With a shake of her head, Becca laughed, saying, "I'm going to just meet you back at the apartment." Feeling conflicted, I looked from Becca to Lucas, rolling my eyes. I gave in and looked back up to Lucas, replying, "Fine, what do you want?" He reached for my hand, as I quickly pulled it back. "Lucas, we are not kids anymore," I said quietly, looking around as people passed by. "Habit," he said. I'm sorry." Rolling my eyes at him, I gestured down the walkway, and began past him.

We both sat down on a bench in the park, just down the street from school and my apartment. Taking a deep breath, Lucas spoke first. "I'm just going to get on with it, okay? Why do you hate me so much? All of these years and you can't even look at me." Sighing, I replied, "Lucas, I don't hate you. I'm just--" Unable to finish my sentence, I look down and pretend to pick nail polish off of my index finger.

Lucas moves closer to me, and I can feel his touch near. "Lucas, don't. Please. I am finally getting to where I can go out without thinking of her, and now you are here, and it's all coming back," I answered.

"Jayda, I can help you if you would just let me," he says softly. Rubbing my face with his hand, I look up to him with a tear in the corner of my eye. Not wanting this closeness, but also not wanting his touch to disappear too soon.

I feel myself lean in just slightly to his hand, as I softly close my eyes. "Jayda," he gasps. It's as if I can feel his heart breaking a little bit as I know mine is. Heat radiates from him as he moves even closer to me. I can feel the connection between us, pulling and pulling us in.

"Lucas, do you know how much regret I have from that night? I didn't want to push you away, but I had to. I had to get away. Too many memories, thoughts, and my dad. Lucas, he was so angry. I lied to him, mom, and Nan," I said. "Jayda, they all knew. They had to have all known. We were never apart, and never too far from one another, even when we were. Jayda, I loved you," he said with a soft smile.

Hearing the words, loved you in the past tense, made a shiver glide through my body. Closing my eyes as a tear slipped out, I sensed he must have read my thoughts, because he quickly replied, "I still, love you." His breathing turned heavy, and his hand shook a bit.

My eyes catch his in a questioning glare. "Love me? It didn't look like you loved me, when you were kissing that girl at the party the other night," I argued, full of attitude now. "So, that is what this is all about?" he asks, anger in his tone. "I was at a party, hanging out with some friends, that was it!" "Lucas, I can't do this," I blurt out. "Do what you want, I'm not yours anymore."

Letting those words sink in, I saw his face change from hope to anger. Had he come to this school thinking he could just pick up where we had left off before everything happened? Had he thought being with me here, away from my dad, and everyone else may help?

Standing up, he looked at me one last time and declared, "Jayda, I love you, and I will always love you. I'm sorry about everything that happened with your mom, I truly am. But, you have to live your life. She would want you to be happy, and while you tell yourself that by you being there, you could have saved her; you know that's not true. The Doctor's told you nothing could have helped. That night, I hated everything about it, all but one thing. The smile on your face when I told you how I felt."

With that said, he spun around, and walked away. Tears began streaming down my face, and as I sat on the bench for what seemed like hours thinking back to my mother, Nan, and my dad. I found my thoughts shift to Lucas, and how my heart ached for him now more than ever. Some may call it hope or fate, but I call it love. What we had was real, and now it is nothing but shattered memories.

Chapter 8

The next week went by, and Lucas and I didn't speak if we saw one another. In class and across campus both times, he just briefly looked at me, and then turned his head away in the other direction. Both times left me feeling empty and sad. Not only had I lost the love of my life, but a best friend, too.

"Jayda, are you okay?" Becca asked as we lay outside on the campus lawn, getting some sun. "I'm fine, Becca," I responded. "Look I'm going to a party tonight, you don't have to come, but I wanted to at least say something to you about it," Becca replied. "Why would I not want to come?" I questioned. "It's at the same frat house we went to when Lucas was there, so the odds of him being there again are pretty good," Becca replied.

Sighing, I thought for a moment before answering. "You know what, I'll go. I'm not going to let Lucas ruin my year. And he's definitely not making decisions for me," I replied, smiling at Becca. The grin on her face was intense as she gave me a high five.

Walking up to the house yet again, only this time knowing I would probably see Lucas, gave me butterflies. Taking a deep breath, I stepped through the doors. Instantly we realized the house was packed. A lot more people were here than last time, and most of the lights were off making it very hard to see across the room from one corner to the next.

Looking around we found a cooler and grabbed a drink out of the ice. Two guys walked up to Becca and me, one seems very interested in her. Small talk and a few drinks later the guys were taking us to dance in the other room.

Music was blasting and while Becca was all for it, I, however, was not. "I think I'll just watch," I said to the guy. Becca and her new friend were already out on the floor dancing across the room.

Feeling a little light-headed, I said to the guy again, only this time louder so he could hear me over the music, "No, really, I'll just stand over here," pushing the guys' hands away from my waist as he moved in closer. Gripping my hips tightly, he pulled me to him even more, rubbing his body against mine. "Stop!" I yelled at him as I tried to push back from his grip. Fumbling with his hands around my waist, I dropped my drink as I took a step back.

Just then, someone gripped the guy's arm that was twisted around my waist, throwing him to the floor, and quickly catching me so I wouldn't fall. Surprised, I gasped as I felt my head spin. Feeling my hands on a hard chest, I looked up to find Lucas staring back at me.

Blinking in confusion as I tried to push back from him I found my mind wandering to his lips. Mixed emotions of anger, sorrow and regret circled in my stomach causing me to instantly feel nauseous. His face was a mix of lust and anger. His jaw was clenched tight, and I could feel heat erupting from his skin.

The guy on the floor stood up and walked back towards us. "What the hell?", he yelled at Lucas. Now the party had gotten quieter, everyone waiting for a fight to break out. Lucas pushed me behind him, but never let go of my hand. "I don't think she wanted to dance," Lucas growled. Becca, now across the room, rushed over towards me. "Are you okay?" she asked. "I'm fine," I whispered, swaying back and forth.

The other guy looked at me as I felt my body heat up and my vision grew blurry. Trying to catch me before it happened, almost as if I was experiencing an out-of-body something, I fell to the ground. "She is all yours," the guy muttered to Lucas as he spun around and disappeared into the crowd.

Music blasted out again, and people began dancing as the guy walked off. Picking me up, Lucas carried me outside while Becca followed behind. Lifting my head, still confused, I felt strong hands on my back and under my legs. I was being carried. Looking up into those eyes, I remembered it was Lucas. Sighing, I closed my eyes and leaned my head on his shoulders as the whispered words left my lips, "I'm sorry."

Opening my eyes, the room was suddenly spinning. Holding my head, the room still spinning, I tried to read the clock. 11:30 am. "Shoot!" I yelled out loud, knowing I had missed my history class. Looking to my nightstand where my phone usually sat, I saw a note from Becca.

I tried to wake you up--no luck. Here's some ibuprofen-take 2, and drink plenty of water drunk girl. Ha! Don't worry about class, I'll give you my notes.

Ps. I know your history and that he is not a killer...so, I didn't make him leave.

Love, your bestie!

Laughing to myself and wondering "Who is not a killer?" in Becca's words. Standing up was terrible and as I tried to make it to the bathroom, I felt sick. Why did I do this to myself? "Damn it, Lucas," I moaned, thinking back to all of those drinks.

Angry with myself that I let my nerves and thoughts with seeing Lucas get the best of me, I huffed out a loud breath. Groaning, I closed my eyes and tried to remember the night.

Looking on the floor I saw a guy's T-shirt covered in what I was pretty sure was my own vomit. "Ugh, the smell," I thought, quickly grabbing my stomach. Getting into the bathroom I turned the water on and stepped into the steaming hot shower. Closing my eyes, I thought back to the note. "What was Becca talking about?" I asked myself again.

Stepping out of the shower, I thought I heard something. Shaking the towel through my hair, I flipped my head back up and screamed when I saw a man standing in the doorway.

Startled, he stumbled backward. "Damn, Jayda, it's me." He chuckled. "Lucas!" I yelled. Watching his eyes roam down my body, I quickly remembered I was only wearing a towel. Looking back to him he wore a pair of faded jeans low on his hips with no shirt, showcasing his muscular build and tan chest.

Licking my lips, I tried to catch my breath. "Lucas, what the hell are you doing?" I screamed at him. "And why are you here?" I asked. Catching him staring at me yet again, I narrowed my eyes and grimaced. "Lucas!" I yelled again, cutting off his thoughts, and bringing his mind back to the conversation.

"Sorry, yes. I helped you back here last night, and well, you didn't want me to leave. So, I stayed," he replied. "Where did you sleep?" I quickly asked. He hesitated before answering with a sly grin, "With you," he smirked.

My eyes went wide and panic instantly set in. "I'm kidding, Jayda, I slept on the couch," he said with a chuckle and walked back out the door. "Lucas," I said in a soft tone. "Why did you come back here?" I asked.

Turning back around and walking a little closer, he answered, "Because, I wanted to be sure you were okay, and when I went to leave, you asked me to stay with you. I laid with you in the bathroom for a bit, and then when I knew you were fine, I carried you back in here," he answered.

"What happened to your shirt?" I questioned. "Let's just say an awkward moment," he replied. "What awkward moment?" I questioned. "You tried to kiss me," he said, boasting, full of pride. Groaning, I rubbed my face, full of embarrassment, and closed the door as he walked out.

Lucas was sitting on the couch as I walked into the room. Seeing me, he sat up, locking his gaze to mine. Before I sat down I asked, "Did you kiss me back?" Thinking about my question, he replied, "No. You tried to kiss me but then threw up all over my chest. I took my shirt off and then wiped it up."

I dropped my face in my hands. "I'm so sorry, Lucas, I'm so sorry," I said. Laughing he replied, "It's fine, and that's basically what you kept saying last night, and I told you, it was fine then, too."

Sitting down next to him I just shook my head. Letting my shoulders fall a bit, I said, "Thank you for helping me last night. I never act like that, but for some reason I let Becca talk me into moving out of my comfort zone." Looking back at me, he smiled before replying, "I would do it all again, you know that." Sighing, I asked, "Why are you always so good to me?" Looking into his eyes, I swear I saw a hint of sparkle as he replied, "You know why."

Getting up from the couch, I walked over to the kitchen and asked, "Do you want me to cook you breakfast?" "No, I am going to go, but thanks," he said. "What about your shirt?" I asked as I bit my lip, staring at his tone chest yet again. "What about my shirt?" he replied, looking down to his chest. "Well, you don't have one," I chuckled. "You can't walk across campus without a shirt on." Looking confused, he replied, "Why can't I?." "What?" I said with wide eyes.

He walked around the kitchen island and stopped right in front of me. Feeling him so close made me a little nervous as I felt butterflies in my stomach. "You jealous someone will see me, Jayda?" he asked in that tone that made me weak for him.

Dropping my head, unable to look him in his eyes, I replied, "No, not at all. I just hate for you to not have a shirt when it's my fault in the first place. Go for it!" I reply, nodding to the door.

Taking a step back, he walks to the door and opens it. Looking back at me he says my name. Looking back up, I see in his eyes the young boy I fell in love with years ago. "Thanks for last night," he says with a mischievous grin. Rolling my eyes, I just shake my head and smile.

Watching the door close, I think back to all the times he made me feel like he just did. His goofy comments, but his heartfelt moments where I knew he would never let anything happen to me.

Chapter 9

"So, I see your mystery man is gone," Becca says as she walks into the room, tossing her bag on the table. Sitting down, I slide the bag of chips I'm eating to her. "Take these, please, before I eat my weight in these dang chips."

Laughing, she grabs a handful and then rolls the bag closed. "So, how did it go?" she asks. Looking at her with sadness on my face, feeling as if I've lost Lucas all over again, tears form in my eyes.

"Jayda," she says sadly, standing up and hugging me. Tearful, I shake it off and stand up. "I'm fine. It's just hard to see him again after everything." "Jayda, why do you feel like you two can't be together?" she asks. "You two can at least try to talk."

Thinking about her question, I answer honestly. "I think when my mom died, I blamed him for me not being there. Then with my dad being angry with him as well, I used that as my punching bag, too. He was easy to blame, and even though deep down I knew nothing was his fault, I took all of my hurt out on him.

After some time, I felt so guilty that I didn't have the strength to apologize to him, and pushing him away got my mind off of losing her." Becca walked over, hugging me again. "They say you hurt the people you love most," she says. "You know, when something happens in your life, you tend to take it out on those closest to you. I think that's what you did with Lucas, and I think he has already forgiven you."

Sighing, I wipe the tears from my face. "You should have seen him with you last night. Jayda, that boy is crazy about you. You were a hot mess, all over the place, and he knew exactly what to do and say to get you to calm down. I came back to your room to check on you, and you were curled up on his chest, sound asleep. I asked him several times if he needed anything, and he just smiled and said, No, he had you."

As Becca disappeared from my room I smiled at the words he had said to her. I could just picture him saying that. Lucas was always in control of whatever was going on, especially when it involved me. Sighing, I picked up my phone and dialed his number, just needing to hear his voice.

A women's voice answered. Looking at the number to be sure it was Lucas, I said, "Who is this?" The voice said, "Hello?" I hung up. Furious, but trying to not let it affect me, I closed my eyes and fell back on my bed trying to keep the tears from falling.

Three missed calls from Lucas when I looked at my phone later that afternoon. Shaking my head when his number appeared on my phone yet again, I tossed it on my bed.

"Jayda, I'm leaving," Becca said from the other side of my door. She was going out on a date with the guy she had met at the party. "Have fun!" I called back, getting up off of my bed to change my clothes. Hearing the door close I thought about Lucas and what he was doing tonight, and who he would be with.

Wiping a tear from my cheek I had just pulled on my sweatpants and tossed on a hoodie when my door swung open. Screaming, I threw my hairbrush that was in my hand as hard as I could at the figure. I saw it fly across the room and hit Lucas right in the face.

"What the hell, Jayda?" he yelled. "Lucas!" I screamed again. "What are you doing, and why are you in my apartment?" I questioned. "Relax, Becca let me in when she was leaving. I was walking up to the door when she was walking out. "And she just let you in?" I asked, glaring at him now. "Well, kind of," he smugly answered. "Lucas?" I scolded.

Picking up the hairbrush and rubbing the red mark on his head, he tossed it at me before replying, "I told her that you called me, and needed me to stop by so we could chat. She smiled, so I asked her if I could come on in to surprise you," he sheepishly admitted. "She thought it was sweet," he replied with a grin.

"Lucas, there is nothing about sneaking into my apartment and almost catching me changing, sweet," I asked sharply. "When were you changing?" he questioned with heated eyes. "Just now," I said with a high pitched voice. "Dang, a few minutes late," he teased. "Lucas!" I yelled again. "You wouldn't answer my calls, so I came over. Now that I know where you live, I took full advantage of it," he said. Shrugging my shoulders, I closed my eyes and rubbed my face.

"Can you please just leave?" I asked calmly. "No, I'm not," he said in a rude tone. Jumping on my bed he spread out his legs, putting his arms behind his head, and making himself comfortable. "Get out!" I shouted. "No!" he said sternly. "Damn it, Lucas, I'm not playing. We are not kids anymore, and I'm not playing these stupid games. Get out of my room, now!"

Standing up, he glared at me, getting right in my face, "What happened to my Jayda, my best friend?" he asked. "When you find her, tell her to give me a call."

Surprised by his comment, I replied, "I'm not sure, but I'm sure you could make better use of your time in someone else's apartment," I sneered in response. Laughing, he grabbed me by the shoulders and pushed me slowly back up to the bedroom wall. "Just so we are clear, the girl you are so mad about that answered my phone, was actually my roommate's girlfriend," he sneared.

Breathing heavy, I felt my face pale, and in a quick second he was dropping his hands from my shoulders, and heading for the door. "Lucas!" I called to him. "What Jayda, What?" he shouted as he turned back around with frustration on his face.

I didn't' even think about it. I just ran to him, with tears filling my eyes. I had pushed him away for so long, and I just couldn't do it anymore. Practically tackling him at the door, I crashed my lips to his as he wobbled backwards, but held onto me tightly.

As soon as I felt his arms wrap around me and kiss me back, I let go of all thoughts. I only thought about how good it felt to have him hold me again. His kisses were just as eager as mine, and neither of us were ready to stop. It was like a frenzy of old and new lust, combined with mixed regret, and new desires.

Chapter 10

A knock at my door woke me up. Looking at the window, I saw that it was morning. "Jayda, you can't miss class again. Get up!" Becca's voice rang out. Looking at my phone, the clock said 8:45am. "Crap!" I said to myself, sitting up, knowing class started in an hour.

Looking over across the bed, I saw Lucas lying next to me, moving around. Turning over, he smiled up at me with messy hair, and a cheesy grin. "Good morning," he said gruffly, sitting up and pulling me to him. "Hi," I answered softly as my rosy cheeks broke out in a huge grin. Kissing him was so easy. Falling for your best friend is easy. We knew each other almost better than we knew ourselves.

We had stayed up most of the night talking, and trying to make up for lost time. Apologies after apologies, followed by mostly me, crying, followed by a lot of making up, kept us pretty busy. Remembering the night, Lucas grinned back at me as Becca knocked again on the door. "Jayda, are you okay? Did you and Lucas talk?" she asked, standing on the other side. "I hope it was okay I let him in? Are you mad?" she questioned in a worried tone.

"She's not mad!" Lucas yelled. Looking directly to me as he said it. Red hot embarrasement coursed through my body, all the way to my toes. "Lucas!" I scolded, as I pulled the sheet up over my head, as if I needed to hide. "Oh, my-- well hello, Lucas," Becca's voice said from the other side. I could just hear the grin in her tone. "Hi, Becca," he answered with a laugh. "I'll just meet you both there," she giggled back, and rushed out the door.

The next few weeks Lucas and I spent almost every second we could together, as if we had never even been apart. We still both had regrets from the past few years that tended to catch us up in bickering spats, but who doesn't' argue every now and then?

I had just sat down on the couch when there was a knock at the door. Knowing Becca had already left with Dane for the night, I assumed it was Lucas. Opening the door, I gasped. "Dad, hey! What are you doing here?" I asked, surprised to see my father standing in the door. His face didn't exactly look pleasant, but he still smiled and hugged me as he walked in.

Looking around the apartment he replied, "Can't a father surprise his daughter at school?" Smiling, I leaned in for another hug, happy to see him, but also worried because Lucas would be here any minute. Sitting down on the couch, he began small talk, asking me how school was.

I saw that he didn't have a bag with him, and last year when he had visited, he had called and booked a hotel room for the night way in advance. Curious as to why he had made this unexpected visit, I swallowed and took a deep breath before I even asked him.

"Is everything okay?" I asked. "Is Nan fine?" Looking worried now as I rubbed my hands together. "Yes, yes, she is fine. Everything is good," he replied. "My question is, how are you? Meet any new friends lately?" he questioned?

Looking up, I caught the hurt in his eyes. It was the same disappointment I saw the night my mother had passed. He had not only been in shock from her passing, but torn up that I had snuck out, and had been sneaking around with Lucas.

Nan tried to talk to him, and even Lucas's parents said they had thought we were together, but none of that seemed to help. He was dead set on being completely against it. He said it wasn't because it was Lucas- he liked Lucas. It was the deceit I had shown during a time we would never get back. Lucas and I had broken his trust.

Another knock at the door broke my thoughts, whipping my head up to the door as it swung open. "Babe, I'm here." Lucas's voice rang out. Walking through the door, Lucas had not even closed it and my father was already standing up tall in disgust, glaring at us both.

Lucas halted with a surprised look on his face. I felt like I was reliving that moment years ago as I looked at my father's face. The room was spinning, and the two people I loved most in the world now disliked each other even more.

Lucas continued to walk towards me as he approached my father with his hand out, "Sir, it's been a long time." Dad didn't even look at him, he just walked past him, looking back to me with dissappointment. Looking back to Lucas my father said, "I ran into your parents and they told me you had transferred here a few months back. I wasn't stupid. I knew why. I just didn't know why once again, I was the last to know." Lucas stepped forward, "Sir, I love your daughter, and you know I always have."

"I don't want to hear it, Lucas. Here we are again with both of you lying to me," he yelled back, with a grave expression on his face. "Son, I have known you since you were a toddler. Do you think I didn't see how you looked at her all those years? I wasn't dumb, Lucas. I know you loved her, but not one time did you make any effort to talk to me about it. Instead, you go behind my back not only once, but twice now.

Is it not enough that you two broke our families apart already once, and then your mother?" he replied, choking up, and dropping his head to the floor. Looking back up with hurt in his eyes, he just shook his head and began to walk out the door.

"Dad," I yelled, reaching for him as Lucas pulled me back. Looking to Lucas with frustration, his jaws were clenched and fists at his side. "Sir, that's not true. We did nothing to break up our families. If anyone did, it was you," Lucas sternly argued back to my father. "Lucas!" I yelled, looking back at him.

Turning around, my father's expression looked cold. He said nothing and slammed the door behind him. Running to the door, Lucas grabbed me again. "Let me go, Lucas!" I yelled. "No, he's not right, Jayda. He knows he's not right," he said. "Let him go and calm down. We will talk to him another time about everything," he pleaded, still holding my hand.

Shaking him off with furry in my eyes, I pushed him away from me. "I can't believe you said that to him," I huffed out, breathing heavy as tears filled my eyes. "Just go, Lucas! Just go. I can't talk to you right now. I have to find my dad," I said to him, pointing to the door.

Lucas took a deep breath and walked to the door, turning back around. "Jayda, If I leave right now, you are letting me go. I won't try this again," he said with pain in his eyes. Confused and angry, I shook my head and brushed past him, out the door to find my dad who we had once again destroyed.

Chapter 11

Has there ever been a time when you have done something so irrational that years later you wonder how you even managed to do something as such? Thinking back to that day in my apartment, I sometimes wonder what would have happened if I would have just stayed there, with Lucas. If I would not have chased after my dad and would have just let him go calm down as Lucas had put it.

If I would not have gone home that weekend to find out Nan had gotten sick. While my dad was furious with me about Lucas and yet another lie, he was lost at what to do, watching our family fall apart all over again.

I remember walking through the front door and seeing Nan on our couch, coughing and confused as to why I was there. Looking at my dad's face when I knew he had been lying to me all these months about her. He had come to see me at school because he had found out about Lucas, yes, but he had also come to tell me Nan was not doing well.

Just three years ago my life was completely flipped inside out, yet again. How much hurt can a person take in a lifetime? "Not that much," I thought to myself, as I answered my phone. "Hey Dad, how are you doing?" "Hey sweetie, I'm great! Are you still up for meeting me today for lunch?" he asked. "Sure, I'll see you at the café," I replied. Hanging up the phone, I looked around at my office and the blank walls. Sighing, I thought back to the past few years.

I had done it. I had left school three years ago to go back home. I finished my semester of classes on-line, thanks to my amazing teachers understanding my family situation. Becca was furious with me at first, but eventually, she got over it, and we stayed in touch over the years.

Transferring back home to our local College, I finished my business degree. Lucas had called and sent a few messages from time to time during that first year, but generally, they were short and simple asking about Nan and how she was doing.

That year was a struggle for us all. Nan had cancer, and I had just lost the love of my life, not even fighting for him. I just gave up, yet again. Lucas deserved someone who knew how to handle more than what was right in front of her.

Walking into the café I spotted my dad smiling back at me, holding an envelope in his hand. "Hey!" he said, standing up and hugging me. Over the past few years, we had mended our relationship. We both started seeing a counselor about my mother's death, and currently we still each met with her on occasion.

I had cut my visits back to only every other month, but my father had kept his monthly visits. He had apologized several times for how he treated Lucas, and how he had handled the situation. He knew that a lot of the things he had said over the years were out of spite due to the anger he held inside from mom's death, but he also was upset I had lied.

He had tried to mend things with Lucas's family, and even though it took time, they were happy to let us back into their lives. Lucas never came home after College. He moved away to start a job in LA. I occasionally heard things from his parents or through dad from time to time, but usually, I tried to block out the thoughts because it hurt too much to think about him.

After Nan passed, he never reached out anymore, nothing more to say I guess. From time to time he would come home to visit his parents, but we never saw him, and they never invited us over while he was there.

I remember one night, I heard something on my window. Rushing over and thinking it may be him, only to find a bird. I cried myself to sleep that night. When my dad asked me the next day why I looked so sad with bloodshot eyes, I told him I just missed Nan. While I did miss her so very much, my heart longed for Lucas.

"You okay?" dad asked as we sat down. "Yes, I'm fine, just hungry," I said, shaking off the memories. "Did you order?" I asked. "No, I thought we could talk a bit before we do if that's okay?" he asked. "Sure, I have an hour for lunch, so what's up?" I asked, looking confused at his expression while he still held the envelope.

"I have something from Nan to give you," he said. Looking up from the menu, I asked, "What is it?" Nan had passed almost two years ago, and while she had lived with us for years, Nan was always very private about her own things. She still did her own finances and helped pay bills while living with my parents.

"Nan bought a cottage in Sanibel shortly after you left for College. She knew how much you loved going there, and after I sold our beach house, she wanted you to always feel like you still had a place to escape to," he replied. "Okay," I said slowly. Why didn't you ever tell me this, and why now?" I asked him. "Did you sell it?" I questioned. "No," he answered. "She left it to you," he replied, handing me the envelope. "Everything you need to know is in here, and any questions you have, just call the number in there and he can help you. She wanted you to have it." Dad smiled as he handed it all over across the table.

Still confused about the news, I reached out to take the envelope. I begin to open it and see a note from her written in her handwriting. Immediately tearing up, I close the envelope, knowing I can't read it here.

"Why are you just now giving me this?" I ask, looking back up to him. "She had asked me to wait until you finished with College. You had been so busy, I just thought I would give you some time," he said softly. "I have never been there, and I only know it is close to where ours used to be," he said, taking a deep sigh. Memories flashed back to him as they were to me.

Smiling at him, I stood up. "Dad, I need to go. I'm not really hungry any longer," I say to him, trying all I could do to hold in the tears. Nodding, he understood. As he kissed me goodbye, he whispered, "I love you so much." Leaning back, I hugged him again replying, "I love you too, dad."

Chapter 12

A few days had gone by and I still couldn't read the letter from Nan. So many thoughts spun in my mind about how she did this. Going back to Sanibel was something I often thought about, but I had lost so much there, too.

When my dad sold our beach house I figured I would never see that beach again. A few years after, I asked him if he was going to buy a beach house somewhere else and he replied, "A beach is no longer a place for me." I remember crying in my room all night because I loved it so much.

Picking up the mail, I smiled when I saw an invitation from Becca. Opening it up, my grin grew as I read the words. It was her wedding invitation, and it was beautiful. Becca and Dane had stayed together through college, and while I was no longer there, we had spoken weekly.

Dane and Lucas were in the same fraternity, and over the years they had become good friends. From time to time Becca would mention his name, never too much because she knew I didn't want to hear it. Sometimes his name would slip through stories and every time my heart would break.

Sticking the invite on my refrigerator, I looked over to my closet where the dress hung. I was her maid of honor, and while I was so excited to share on her special day, I was not eager to see Lucas.

The morning had been perfect. Becca was gorgeous, and Dane catered to her as always, sending her a note before the ceremony. Hugging the Bride to be I wiped a tear from the corner of my eye, full of excitement for her and in awe. "You look so beautiful," I admitted. Smiling back at me, she grinned and replied, "I'm so glad you are here with me."

Watching her mother help her put on her dress was a little tough. The two were laughing and hugging, it was so very sweet, yet a reminder of what I would never have. Everyone was getting dressed and putting their final touches on when I stepped out of the door for some fresh air. Walking across the hall to the patio doors, I opened them quickly and stepped out, taking a deep breath, trying to ease my mind and nerves.

Becca and Dane had decided to get married in the hometown we went to College in, where they had met. Being back here brought back so many memories, but that was all in the past, and I had told myself years ago that I just needed to move forward, and leave that all behind me.

Opening my eyes, I smiled, thinking of how far I had come from that young, naive girl. How my therapist had helped me understand that some things in life you cannot control, while others you can. The past should not define your future; closing certain doors only allow you to open new ones.

Closing my eyes and settling my thoughts, I opened them only to find myself gasping. I saw him- Lucas. He was walking arm in arm with a tall Blonde who looked like she was out of a Glamour magazine. She strutted with a smile and looked amazing in a tight, lilac dress.

Gulping, I felt my chest raise a little with jealousy, shouting inside with tears. He wasn't mine, and I had made that clear more than once years ago. I felt myself jump back from the railing, trying to get out of sight so he couldn't see me, but I saw his eyes look up briefly as I turned quickly around and walked back in.

Throughout the ceremony, I had goosebumps knowing that while I stood up in front of everyone, Lucas was able to see me. Swallowing a few times out of nervous habit, and then catching a few tears while Becca and Dane said their vows, I looked out into the crowd and spotted him staring directly at me. Quickly looking away, I smiled at Becca as I handed back her bouquet of Pink and yellow roses.

My nervous energy wanted to shoot out of my body, fingers shaking, and my breaths deep. It was all so much, but I had to keep that fake smile on for the sake of Becca's big day. Seeing him sitting there looking handsome as ever, made my belly flip and my heart cringe.

The reception hall was beautiful as we walked in. The lights shined bright, and light classical music played while we ate. We said our speeches, I teared up only twice during mine, and of course, Dane's best man, Brady, hazed him as much as possible, giving the crowd many laughs.

I sat there watching their first dance together, so happy for my friend. Becca had been there for me through a lot. She had been the friend that helped me through my anger after my mother's death, and she had been there for me after Lucas. Becca was truly an amazing person, and I caught myself smiling in her direction, completely happy for her and Dane.

Seeing they were almost done, I stood up and began to walk out on the floor. Becca and Dane had asked the bridal party to dance with them at the end of their first dance. Brady was my dance partner, and also the best man.

He and Dane were in the same fraternity together. He and I knew each other well from school, but over the years, we too had drifted apart. The only time I saw him was when I went to visit Becca and Dane, and Brady would join us for the night.

"Well, don't you look amazing in that dress," he said in a mischievous tone. Chuckling, I took his hand and began to dance. "Watch it, I may accidentally step on your toes," I replied with narrowed eyes. Spinning me around, he chuckled and pulled me in closer as we all danced around Becca and Dane.

All eyes were on the dance floor, and thanks to the bright lights shining on us I could barely see when I looked out to the crowded room. The song ended, and as if right on cue, a fast song began. The bridal party busted out in cheers, hoots, and hollers. We all began to dance around the newlyweds as laughter erupted from the people watching us.

I looked at Becca and she was smiling, full of laughter as Dane swung her around in his arms. A hand grabbed mine again, pulling me into a tight chest. Looking up, I saw Brady smiling at me with those easy eyes. Scrunching my nose at him, I continued to dance and enjoy the night.

Chapter 13

A few songs later and many drinks in, I sat down to catch my breath as Brady had gone to grab us a few drinks of water. Becca and Dane had just walked off to begin greeting more people and thanking them for coming.

Looking up as I fixed my heel strap, a bottle water was shoved in my face. "Thanks Brady," I began to say, but stumbled on my words when I saw who had handed it to me. "Lucas!" I gasped in surprise. "Hey, Jayda, how are you?" he asked. "Hi, I'm good, thanks." I tried to say between my coughing spasm and a cool drink of water.

Finally catching my breath and calming myself down so I didn't make a complete fool of myself, I asked, "How's your new job?" "It's a job," he replied, looking at me, almost seeming dejected by the question.

Looking up at him, I felt my heart peel away at the silence, thankful I saw Brady walking up to us. Putting his hand out he said, "Lucas, good to see you man."

Lucas looked between the two of us and returned the hand shake. "Hey Brady, how are you." "Doing good, just trying to teach this lady here how to dance without stepping on people's feet," he answered with a laugh. I smiled at Brady, and then looked back to Lucas seeing that he didn't seem to find it amusing.

Just then his date walked up, wrapping her arm around his. "Hi, I'm Stacey. And you are?" Looking to me, and then to Brady. Not introducing us, Lucas muttered, "Stacey, these are some friends of mine from College. It was good to see you all." With that, he turned around with her arm still on his and walked away.

Watching him leave with her and only saying a few words, made a sick feeling rise in my stomach. He looked so cold. His words were sharp, and his jaw tight. Swallowing and taking a deep breath, I closed my eyes and wished the time to quickly pass by.

The rest of the night went just as smooth as the day had. As the crowd got smaller, the dancing got a little crazier, and the music louder. Mostly friends from College, and friends both Dane and Becca had made along the way, filled the dance floor and bar area.

Pointing a finger at Brady, I laughed until I snorted awkwardly. "No, it's your fault," I yelled. Throwing his hands back, he shouted, "Wait a minute now, just wait.

You were the one that knocked it over, I had nothing to do with that first part," he stated, as he laughed out loud.

Becca and Dane who were now walking over to us jumped in on the conversation. "Brady is trying to say he had nothing to do with the night at the Diner," I said, a little too loudly. Becca's eyes shot up, glaring at Brady. "That is a lie, she argued with a laugh. "You were the one that pushed Jayda into the jar," she accused. Dane, who was now trying to defend his friend, laughed as Lucas and his date walked up.

Looking at all of us as Becca turned her nervous eyes to me, I just smiled. "Well, hello there," I said to them. Brady and Dane shot each other a look as Lucas asked, "What's going on? Why is Jayda being so loud? Or has she just had a little too much to drink. She can do that from time to time." Lucas teased, but not too subtle in the point he was trying to make.

The group went silent as Brady narrowed his eyes at him, ready to defend me. Dane laughed, pushing Lucas in the arm. "Shut up, man. Jayda is trying to weasel her way out of a story. Becca began laughing, seeming to try to lighten the mood a little. "Well, let's hear it then," Lucas says to Brady with a smile. His date Stacey just glared at me in disgust.

"A few months ago, Jayda came to visit Becca and Dane. We had all went out and had a few drinks. We stayed out pretty late, and at the end of the night, Becca and Jayda swore they needed cheese fries. We went to the diner down the street from the bar, and when we walked in, there was a huge jar of gumballs by the register. The entire time they ate they talked about how gross that jar was because people could just reach their dirty hands in, and grab out a piece of gum with no wrapper.

When we left, Jayda tripped and pushed the jar all over the floor, spilling it everywhere. The waitress was furious, and swore she did it on purpose. Jayda swears I pushed her into the counter, but she fell all on her own," Brady said, looking to Jayda with a wink. Jayda just smirked, and shook her head.

Setting my glass down, I tossed my hands up in the air. "Fine, I fell into the counter, okay?" I argued, shaking my hands into fists. Laughter from Becca and Dane erupted as Brady slowly clapped. "Brady!" I screamed, as everyone else other than Lucas, laughed. "Okay, okay. It's time to come clean," Brady replied, casually looking around the group.

Dane chuckled as Becca hit his arm. "I may have slightly pointed you into the direction of that jar," he said. "Brady! I knew it," I said as I took a few steps towards him, but tripped over the table cloth. Slipping in the other direction, I put my hand back hoping to catch myself, but two strong hands quickly caught my back, breaking my fall. Looking up, I was practically cradled in Lucas's arms with him staring right at me.

It was as if time stood still, and the only two people with pounding hearts were he and I. His date stood a few steps behind him as Brady just looked flustered. Becca and Dane just stared at us with wide eyes, almost bracing for the aftermath.

Still, just holding me, I wiggled out of his hands and fixed my dress, wiping at the front. Taking off my heels, I whispered quietly, "Thanks, Lucas." I guess I am a little clumsy." His eyes stared back at me and he had no words, now just a few steps away from one another. I could feel my heart pounding in my chest, and his breaths were erratic.

Clearing his throat, Dane asked, "How about another dance before we shut this place down?" Grabbing Becca's hand, and spinning her to the dance floor, she laughed as the group began to break up.

Brady reached for my hand and I took it, following him back to the floor. Looking over my shoulder, I could see Lucas staring at me while his date glared at him. He looked as if he was just about to say something, but then turned around, and took a drink from the table.

Waiting outside for the Uber driver, I sat on a bench looking at the photos on my phone I had taken from the day. Scrolling up farther, I moved my finger too quickly causing an older group of photos to appear on the screen.

Suddenly, I came to an old picture of Lucas I had kept for many years, never having the courage to delete it. On my bad days, I tended to open it up and remember his smile. He and I were sitting on the beach, I leaned back on his chest between his legs, smiling wide, while his hands were wrapped around me. We were both so in love and had nothing pulling us apart.

A horn honked and caught me by surprise, causing me to drop my phone to the ground. Reaching for it, a hand beat me to it. Looking up, I saw Lucas standing in front of me, holding my phone. "Here," he said. Gazing up at him as he stood there alone, I asked in a snippy tone, "Where's your girlfriend?" "Where's Brady?" he countered.

Rolling my eyes, I stood up and as he handed me back my phone, he looked at the picture on the screen. Embarrassed, I quickly snagged it from him, tucking it into my purse. "We were happy back then, weren't we? Not a care in the world, but each other," he said. A sick feeling in my gut spun around, and I had no words. His eyes were full of heat, but I couldn't tell if they were full of anger or longing.

"Brady isn't my boyfriend," I replied quickly. Looking behind him, I saw Brady, Dane, and Becca were awaiting our ride, each looking our way with questions. "Well, I sent my so-called, girlfriend home already," he replied, still staring at me with heated eyes.

For a split second, I thought about how it would feel to be in his arms again. How his kiss would feel, and how we could make this work. But, instead, I smiled and just said, "It was really good to see you, Lucas." I took a deep breath, and made myself walk away to the driver who had just arrived to pick us all up.

Chapter 14

Dane and Becca had blocked off rooms at a hotel for any guests traveling out of town to stay in. They had stayed in the Bridal suite, and were taking off first thing in the morning for their two-week honeymoon to Italy.

Brady had walked me to my room last night, but he didn't try to kiss me. I think he knew we would always just be good friends. He had an early flight out to Dallas for work, so he was leaving at 6am. Giving me a friendly kiss on the cheek at my door was all that he left me with. As I watched him walk down the hall, I thought to myself at how I wished he too, would find love, but unlike me, maybe he could understand how to hang out to it.

Walking into the breakfast area the next morning, I went straight for the coffee. With the night I had, and all of the thoughts that kept me up, I knew I needed it. I tossed and turned all night, reliving some of my greatest and worst memories, all involving Lucas. Eyeing a blueberry muffin, I grabbed it and continued walking through the breakfast line.

Turning around with my muffin and a cup of coffee, I looked at the tables for a spot to sit. Most were taken or being saved, but a few were open with people I recognized from the wedding. Looking to the corner of the room I saw Lucas, sitting alone with an empty chair at a small round table.

Looking up, he saw me and smiled. Looking to the empty chair he shrugged his shoulders, almost as if he were inviting me over, but letting me decide. Taking a deep breath, I knew I shouldn't, but seeing him sitting there caused me to want just a few more moments with him before once again, we walked away from one another.

"Good morning, sunshine." He said, while smirking up at me. "How did you sleep, or did you get any?" he sarcastially asked. "I got plenty of sleep," I replied in a snarky tone. "Plenty of sleep, alone." I answered slowly, watching his jaw tighten, trying to hide his grin.

"So, where is your girlfriend?" I asked, while pretending to look around. "She is not my girlfriend, and she only attended the wedding with me last night as a friend. I told you, I sent her home after the wedding," he answered sharply.

Confused, I raised my eyebrows at him. "She's an old friend from College that I asked to attend the wedding with me, and then I got her a ride home at the end of the night," he replied, looking at me as if he were trying to read my thoughts. "Oh, well why did you bring a date?" I questioned. "Because, I thought you probably had one," he honestly answered, catching me off guard.

Gently setting his cup down, he just stared at me. Speechless, I took a bite of my muffin. "Well, I didn't," I replied. "Brady is just a good friend, and always has been. We had a good time at the wedding, but my night ended when he walked me to the door.

As the breakfast area began to get crowded, I finished my muffin and began picking up my things. Both of us silently looked from one another, then around the room. Unspoken words and regrets lingered, but neither of us knew where to begin. Both of us jealous and unable to contain the attraction for the other.

Sighing, I finally said, "Well, I am going to head out." "Jayda," he said softly, moving his hand across the table to touch mine. I flinched at his touch and gently pulled back from him. "Lucas," I said in a timid tone. "It was really good to see you." Rubbing the back of his neck, he smiled, and sat back in his chair. "Good to see you, Jayda. You looked beautiful last night," he replied. Smiling softly at him, I looked into his eyes for what seemed like minutes before I replied, "Thank you. You were pretty handsome yourself."

Reaching back across the table he lightly rubbed a finger over my wrist. His touch was enough to cause my mind to instantly stop thinking, and just be in the moment. Not wanting this moment to end, I paused before saying, "Well, Goodbye, Lucas." With a heavy sigh, I stood up from the table and smiled at him. He would always have my heart, this I knew, but I was not allowed to have his. I was not deserving of it again.

Walking away from him at the table was just another thing I was going to add to my list of regrets. Knowing our lives had taken us in different directions, and while love was strong, sometimes it just wasn't strong enough to withstand the moment or place in time.

Chapter 15

A few months had gone by, and while I thought I may hear from Lucas since seeing him at the wedding, I had not. He hadn't called, texted, or even come home to visit his parents. I hadn't really expected as much, only had hoped deep down fate would work some magic to give me one last chance to make things right again.

I still thought about him everyday as I had for the last several years, but I also felt like staying away was the best thing for him. He deserved so much, and I felt like I had let him down too many times already.

I still hadn't read the letter that Nan had written me, but I had looked into the cottage at Sanibel. It turned out, she had purchased a small beach cottage right on the ocean. It wasn't too far from the beach home we had when I was a child, but far enough away I could create new memories and not be reminded of all the bad ones. It was actually, perfect.

The small cottage sat on the far side of the beach near the big sand dunes where the sea turtles tended to lay eggs. The water washed up many sea shells on that end of the beach, and the shoreline was crisp and clean.

The gentleman at the bank had helped me get everything figured out. She had paid it off, and I owed nothing on it. It was all mine. Smiling at the thought of her watching me in this cottage made me happy. I thought of the new traditions I would want to make here, and how I always wanted to be sure I somehow held onto Nan's spirit.

My dad had helped me get my things moved to the cottage. While he had said he would not return to the beach, he managed to stay for a night with me here and there. I knew it would take him time, but Nan had always said the beach life was in his blood, so I knew he would return.

He had actually asked his therapist out, which made me laugh, because I thought that was illegal or something like that. Hey, as long as he's happy, I was happy for them. She's actually great for him.

Casey, my boss at the magazine company, was so kind. I had told her a little bit about my mother and Nan, and how she left me with the cottage. Casey decided since the office was going through renovations, I could just work remotely for a while and submit my writings monthly to her. While she was understanding from having lost her father at a young age, I was grateful for her compassion.

Picking up the letter my Nan had written me, I walked out to the beach and sat down. Looking out to the water I remembered her smile and laugh. I remembered all of life's lessons she had shared with me.

Closing my eyes, I thought about that little girl and little boy who would race down these sandy shores searching for the biggest seashell. I thought about Nan baking cookies, and while we helped her with the cookie dough, Lucas would eat half of it.

I remembered the way Lucas would look at me when it was just he and I sitting out here, watching the waves. The kisses, the laughter, and the memories we had shared all those years ago. The only times I felt safe and whole, were the moments I was here with him.

I even remembered back to my mother. I thought about her sweet smile, and her golden hair blowing in the breeze as we sat, reading together in the early evenings when I was young. Taking in the ocean air I felt as if I could almost smell the wildflower perfume she wore on special occasions, or the sweet pea candle she would burn throughout the beach house continuously. Laughing to myself, knowing how much my father hated that smell, but never told my mom.

Taking a much needed, deep breath, I opened the letter and began to read.

Jayda,

I am so sorry that I have gone. I am even more sorry I had to leave you alone with your father, lord help him learn to cook so he can feed you.

My sweet girl, I loved you from the moment I saw you in that hospital. I knew then that you had so much going for you, and as you grew, I was lucky enough to watch you grow into a beautiful young lady with a kind soul.

We have had plenty of sadness in our life, and too much for a family such as us if you ask me, but while the hurdles were tough, you carried on. You may not think so my dear, but you were the glue that held it all together.

When you left for College your father was so proud of you, and even more when you came back to help him through my illness. He never wanted to see you fail sweetheart, but he needed you then, and you were there. Always remember that life doesn't make decisions for you, you make them for yourself.

Your mother thought the world of you. She was such a fine woman, and when your father brought her home for the first time, I just knew they would share a lifetime of happiness together. It was a terrible thing that hap-

pened, but you have to know that the best thing you can do to honor her and I, would be to follow your heart, and live out your own life. Don't waste the time that you have here- you never know when it will be up.

Now, I bought a house... Surprise! I know it seems a little much more than a card, or a bicycle. I mean it's a house, I know, but I wanted to leave you with something I knew you could raise a family of your own in, and make memories you would cherish for years to come.

I will always be with you dear, and so will your mother. Give your father time, he'll eventually come back-he loves it there just as much as you do-I told you before, the water is in our blood.

Be sure to get with Harold at the bank, he has everything you need. I hope you love it as much as I hope you do. Every time the waves hit the shore just think of me, and each time you make your very own s'more on the beach, think of your mother. That was one of her favorite things to do with you, too.

Lastly, I will leave you with this. We are given a purpose when we are put here on this earth, so live yours.

I love you so very much.
Xoxo, Nan

Ps. Don't be upset about your other gift- it may not work out, but I have a feeling it just might. Open your heart. I love you.

Folding the letter, tears were streaming down my face, caught up in so much emotion I couldn't contain my cries. Tucking my head into my knees, I sat there on the beach thinking of the words she had written, and how much I missed her and my mother both.

A few hours passed and the sun was beginning to set. I was still very tearful and began thinking about her last words again. *"Don't be upset about your other gift- it may not work out, but I have a feeling it just might."* Unsure of what she meant, I tried to think about all of the possibilities, and where it could be.

I decided I would call Harold at the bank and see if there was something he had forgotten to give me. Standing up, I turned around and froze. Gripping the letter tightly in my hand, I felt as if I couldn't breathe. My heart skipped a few beats, blinking my eyes as more tears fell. I finally spoke, "Lucas?"

Chapter 16

Standing near the dunes, just past the cottage, Lucas stood holding a piece of paper in his hand that was folded up. Sticking it in his pocket, he began to walk towards me. I instantly felt my palms get sweaty, and my nerves took over.

Seeing him there, walking towards me in the very first place he melted my heart, made me realize just how much I had missed him. Meeting him halfway, I stopped as the sea breeze picked up, and the sun was barely over the horizon.

"Lucas, what are you doing here?" I questioned. Just hearing his name roll of of my lips sent a thrill down my spine. He looked just as shocked as I did. "I'm not really sure," he hesitantly said. I came home to see you, and when your dad answered and said you weren't staying there, he invited me in. Honestly, I thought he may tell me to stay away from you, but instead, he apologized for everything. He told me how sorry he was, and how things over the years had gotten out of hand.

I could hear the waves crashing into the shore just barely over his words. The scent of the ocean blew past, and my heart began to pound even faster. So many questions as to why he was here, or why he had even tried to find me swam in my mind. I just listened as he spoke again.

"He also gave me a letter from Nan." Pulling the letter back out of his pocket, he showed it to me. Shocked that Nan had written him a letter, I gasped when I saw her writing. "What?" I said in shock. "Yeah, I was surprised too, I mean, I knew I was one of her favorites, but-" he teased, looking back to me with that grin that instantly melted my heart.

Smiling, I rolled my eyes, putting my own letter back in my pocket. "Well, what did it say?" I asked. He looked to the letter, and then he looked out to the horizon, pausing for just a moment before answering. "It said that she had bought a house, and needed me to come here and take care of it for her. She also gave me a list of things to check on and keep up with," he replied with a smile that grew with each second bigger and wider.

Unsure of his letter, I replied, "Well, that is weird. Why would she want you to take care of it?" Rubbing the back of his neck with his hand, he replied, "You know Nan. Always a step ahead of everyone else," he chuckled. "What else did she say?" I questioned, eager to hear more words spoken by a woman I truly admired.

Stepping closer to me, he reached out for my hand with a look in his eyes that told me everything was about to change. "I think she was telling me to do this," he said softly, as he pulled me to him and crashed his lips to mine.

Lost in the moment, I thought about nothing other than Lucas and I standing in the middle of the beach, falling back in love. The kiss was filled with so much emotion, passion, and the desire to want more.

Pulling him to me even closer I wrapped my arms around him, knowing I could never let go again. His hands were now around my back, picking me up, and lovingly staring into my eyes as he broke the kiss.

Tears streamed down my face as I tried to understand this was not a dream. This was real, he was real. Lucas was my everything, and I wouldn't be dumb enough to let him go ever again. Regardless of the hurt and regret, my new door had opened, and he was standing just inside waiting for me.

Hearing the waves wash to the shore, and seeing the only man I ever loved staring back at me with lust in his eyes, made me realize the only thing that mattered was this. Our bond, the fight that we had given to simply get back here unknowingly.

Smiling down at him, I said as more tears slid down my cheeks," I love you." Gently kissing me on the lips again, he replied softly, "I love you too, Jayda. God, I love you so much." Sliding back down his body and standing between his arms, we stood there in awe at one another as if we couldn't believe we were finally back here, together.

So much hurt had happened at this very place, but only caring about holding onto one another. It was remarkable to think that while the pain and sadness had overshadowed so much, we had finally reached the barrier and broken through. Our love and the journey we had been on had finally proven to be enough.

Lucas kissed the tip of my nose, and then my cheek as he rubbed his hands down my back. Wrapping my arms around his neck I knew at this moment Nan had just sent me my other gift. A gift that didn't come in the shape of a box or form of a letter, but it was in the form of memory. A memory that would shower me with love from this man forever. A memory of the little boy who became my best friend, love of my life, and one day husband on this very beach. Our perfect paradise.

THE END

A Letter to Lucas

Lucas,

My sweet Lucas. You have sure grown into a fine young man. Watching you when you were a little boy gave me so much joy, but watching how you always were with Jayda gave me more. I know that the years have not been pleasant to you both, and we have been through terrible times, but, if there is one thing you can do for me, it is this.

I bought a cottage for Jayda at Sanibel. I need you to visit there over the next few years, and be sure everything is running properly for her there. I know you two may not be on good terms when you are reading this, but I also know you do things at your own pace and will do this for me. Plus, now that I am gone I can haunt you until you listen to me-- always a step ahead son.

Now, you were like a grandson to me all of those years, and I love you so much. I need you to promise me you will not only take care of the cottage for a while, but watch over the love of your life too.

I know you will figure it out. Follow your heart and when she pushes back, be sure to make every moment count.

I love you. Xoxo, Nan

Authors Note

Love is not perfect, nor is it planned. Every story has an ending, but it's the pages in between that make it great. Live your own love story and enjoy the good, bad, and ugly— those perfect and happy moments, outweigh everything else.

More books by the Author

Love on Shore
Love is a Storm

Follow on Instagram @author.ajohnson
Connect on the Website @ ajohnsonpublishing.com